WOOF!

WOF!

WRITTEN BY
ETHLIE ANN VARE

ILLUSTRATED BY ROBOTS

Published by Central Park South Publishing 2023
www.centralparksouthpublishing.com

Layout and Design by Scott Mosher (theambientmind.com)
Illustrations created using Artificial Intelligence

ISBN: Paperback: 978-1-956452-35-8
Hardback: 978-1-956452-36-5
eBook: 978-1-956452-37-2

This book is mostly true.

Some of what the dog said
I might have gotten wrong.

It all started when I was walking to the bookstore to see what was new in Mysteries Thrillers and Science Fiction. Right in front of Bookstar, taking up practically the whole sidewalk, was the East Valley Animal Shelter Dog Adoption Fair. The cages started at Salt 'n' Straw Ice Cream and didn't end until past Urban Outfitters. I tried to squeeze past.

"Hey. This is your dog."

I whipped my head
around. Who said that?

"This one. See?
He matches you."

WOOF!

It was Joey, a boy from my school. He was leaning against the brick wall trying to look tough, but I think he just likes dogs.

"This one" was named Ranger, and he did match me. Ranger had red hair and amber eyes with gold specks, and looked at the world with an expression that said "I don't care if you don't like me, because I don't like you anyway."

WOOF!

I leaned over the cage.

"What kind of dog are you?"
I asked him.

Ranger looked up at me,
put a paw on the bar of his
cage, looked me straight in
the eyes and said "Woof!"

"Wolf!" I tried to tell her I was a wolf. I shouldn't be at a Dog Adoption Fair, because I am not a dog. I am a wolf, wild and free, and I don't belong in a cage.

Still, if I pretend to be a dog, maybe this human with red fur will get me out of here.

WOOF!

The lady in charge of the Dog Adoption Fair said I needed parental permission and twenty-eight dollars to take Ranger home. I texted my dad. I thought he'd say "no" — saying no is three-quarters of a parent's job — but he said the responsibility will do me good and I should ask the lady if they'll take a check.

WOOF!

Also, my name is not Ranger. Ranger is ordinary. I am not ordinary. I will come when people call me Ranger, however, if there is a biscuit involved.

8

WOOF!

They gave me Ranger's license and registration and a leash to walk him home. Except Ranger doesn't walk. He runs. Really fast. And if he sees a skateboarder across the street, he runs after them. He doesn't wait to cross at the corner, either — he just runs, and I don't want to get yelled at for jaywalking. Or get run over, come to think of it.

Yay! Let's go! Faster, little human. Faster!

WOOF!

The first thing Ranger did when we got home was pee on the carpet. The second thing was tear the head off my sister's stuffed sheep. Then he ran away.

I don't think I'm very good at dog ownership. But my dad said he doesn't know where his home is yet, plus he's just a dog being a dog.

I'm just a wolf being a wolf. I marked my territory, and now I'm going to hunt my dinner. Can you smell that? Someone is cooking campfire meat! Right there, in that big cage….

WOOF!

Well, we found Ranger. He was trying to climb the Mayers' chain link fence to get at their barbecue. He snarled at me when I tried to get the leash on him, but I had a handful of Milk Bones and that distracted him long enough for Dad to push him into the car.

Did you know that if you stick your head out the window of a car when it's going 40 miles an hour, it feels like flying? I could do this all day.

Plus, biscuits.

WOOF!

Dad said maybe we should have a dog that was easier to handle. A poodle, or a weiner dog. But I didn't adopt Ranger because he was easy. I adopted him because he was... him.

I scratched Ranger's ears and told him he was a good boy. He gave me another snarl — note to self, do not pet dog while dog is eating — and a low "Woof." But I don't think he'll run away again.

I'm a wolf. I told you. Don't touch my biscuit.

WOOF!

I was wrong. I'm always getting it wrong. Ranger did run away again. I don't know how he got out of the yard. I'm sure I closed the gate.

It took this many tries before I figured out how to get the latch open.

18

WOOF!

He was more than a mile from home when someone found him and called the East Valley Animal Shelter. I had to leave school early to bail him out.

I was just exploring. I didn't bite anyone. I didn't even chase anyone. Mostly. And now I'm back in jail. The people who work here are nice enough, but it smells bad and I have to share a cage with a rat terrier. I don't like dogs much.

WOOF!

The Animal Control officer was frowning when she brought Ranger out to me. "We are not a no-kill shelter, you know," she said. "We try to find a home for every dog, but..." She explained that dogs don't usually get rescued more than two times.

I don't know exactly what the dogcatcher was saying, but I know a Serious Voice when I hear it.

Ranger looks up at me and says "Woof!

I keep trying to explain to the small human that I'm a wolf, and a wolf travels alone. Also - name's not Ranger.

I told Dad what the lady said about how they are "not a no-kill shelter." Which means... well, you get what it means. He said we should change Ranger's name to Lazarus, because he sort of came back from the dead. It's a Bible story.

"Lazarus is hard to pronounce," Bubbie said. "Call him Laszlo."

"Laszlo is hard to spell," Dad muttered, but there is no point muttering at Bubbie.

"He's a dog," said Bubbie. "He can't spell anyway."

Laszlo. Sure, why not? I was willing to try anything, because if he doesn't come when I call, it will be three strikes and you're out.

WOOF!

"Laszlo! Here, Laz! Come!"

He looked up at me. He looked at his supper dish: Kibbles'n'Bits with a piece of bologna on top. He ate the bologna in one bite. Then he looked at me again.

Here's the thing: I don't like dogs much, and I don't like humans much, either. They always want something from me and somehow I'm always doing it wrong. But the small human with fur like mine... she's not bad.

I don't like to cry in front of people. I don't like to cry in front of a dog, either. But...
"Laszlo. Please come, Laszlo. Please."

26

WOOF!

Laszlo, huh? Okay, fine. If it's that important to her,
I can pretend to be a dog.

Laszlo came up to me, looked me right in the eyes...
and licked the tears off my face.

Laszlo never
ran away again.

WOOF!

He never stopped sticking his head out the car window at 40 miles an hour. He never stopped chasing skateboarders, either.

Turns out, being a dog isn't so bad.

He died in his sleep at
the age of 15 1/2, which
is old for a dog and
very, very old for a wolf.

WOOF!

He was never a good dog.

But he was the dog for me.

Laszlo

THE END

About the Author

Author, journalist and screenwriter Ethlie Ann Vare has been recognized for her young-adult non-fiction books (both the American Library and Public Library Association Award), her television writing (Prism Award), and magazine work (Maggie Award.) *WOOF!* is her first picture book, inspired by her love of dogs and computers. Find her at www.ethlieannvare.com

About the Art

The AI art generators that created the stunning images for *WOOF!* were trained to emulate the bold palette-knife oil paintings of Ben Herman, the author's late father. Ben Herman was a noted portraitist and instructor at the Art Students League in New York City. He never got a chance to meet Laszlo in life, but thanks to the magic of artificial intelligence, they now live together on the page.

A portion of the proceeds of this book will be
donated to Los Angeles Animal Services.

CPSIA information can be obtained
at www.ICGtesting.com
Printed in the USA
BVHW060950140323
660406BV00003B/59